Franklin Snoops

From an episode of the animated TV series *Franklin* produced by Nelvana Limited, Neurones France s.a.r.l. and Neurones Luxembourg S.A., based on the Franklin books by Paulette Bourgeois and Brenda Clark.

TV tie-in adaptation written by Sharon Jennings and illustrated by Sean Jeffrey, Mark Koren, Alice Sinkner and Jelena Sisic.

Based on the TV episode *Franklin Snoops*, written by Laura Kosterski.

Kids Can Press acknowledges the financial support of the Ontario Arts Council, the Canada Council for the Arts and the Government of Canada, through the BPIDP, for our publishing activity.

Published in Canada by
Kids Can Press Ltd.
29 Birch Avenue
Toronto, ON M4V 1E2

Published in the U.S. by
Kids Can Press Ltd.
2250 Military Road
Tonawanda, NY 14150

www.kidscanpress.com

Edited by Tara Walker and David MacDonald

Printed in Hong Kong, China, by Wing King Tong Company Limited

This book is smyth sewn casebound.

CM 03 0 9 8 7 6 5 4 3 2 1

National Library of Canada Cataloguing in Publication Data

Jennings, Sharon
    Franklin snoops / Sharon Jennings ; illustrated by Sean Jeffrey ... [et al.].

(A Franklin TV storybook.)
The character Franklin was created by Paulette Bourgeois and Brenda Clark.

ISBN 1-55337-364-2 (bound)

I. Bourgeois, Paulette II. Clark, Brenda III. Jeffrey, Sean IV. Title. V. Series: Franklin TV storybook.

PS8569.E563F719 2003   jC813'.54   C2002-905544-X
PZ7

Kids Can Press is a *l'oRus*™ Entertainment company

Franklin Snoops

Kids Can Press

FRANKLIN could count by twos and tie his shoes. He was curious about lots of things and he loved to ask questions. "Why does it get dark?" he asked his father. "How old is Granny?" he asked his mother. His parents always answered him as best they could. But one day, Franklin was curious about something that was a secret.

Franklin was eating breakfast when Bear's mother came to the door. She whispered something to Franklin's mother and handed her a shopping bag.

"What's in the bag?" asked Franklin.

"It's a secret," his mother replied.

Franklin didn't give up.

"I can keep a secret," he told his mother again and again.

"So can I," she replied each time.

But later that morning, Franklin found out what he wanted to know.

"I ran into Bear's mother," he overheard his father say. "She'd like you to wrap Bear's birthday present for her."

"Aha!" cried Franklin. "So *that's* what's in the bag!"

Soon, Franklin had another question.

"Why did Bear's mother give you his birthday present?"

"She was afraid that Bear might snoop," explained Franklin's mother.

"*I'd* never snoop," declared Franklin.

His mother smiled.

"Of course not," she said.

At lunchtime, Franklin had an idea.

"Can I wrap Bear's present?" he asked. "I'm really good at wrapping."

His mother laughed.

"I know you are," she agreed. "But I've already wrapped it. Now you will be just as surprised as Bear."

Franklin sighed.

In the afternoon, Beaver phoned and asked Franklin to play baseball. He found his bat in the toy box and searched the hall closet for his glove. And there, hidden behind skis and skates, was a yellow gift bag.

"Bear's present!" he exclaimed.

Franklin grabbed the bag. Then he put it down.
Maybe I shouldn't snoop, he told himself.
Franklin looked at the bag again.
A little peek can't hurt, he decided. As long as
I don't tell Bear.

Franklin pulled out the present.

"A Power Pal!" he exclaimed. "Bear will be so excited!"

Franklin put the gift back in the closet and ran off to play with his friends.

At the park, everyone was talking about what to get Bear for his birthday.

"I know what his mother got him," said Franklin. "But I can't tell you. It's a secret."

"You have to tell us," said Beaver. "That way we won't buy him the same thing."

Everyone agreed with Beaver.

Franklin thought for a moment. Then he told his friends about the Power Pal.

"Wow!" said Snail. "I'll get him the Power Pal Submarine."

"And I'll get him the Power Pal Spacerider," decided Beaver.

"We can all get him Power Pal toys," said Rabbit.

The next day, Franklin and his mother went to
the toy store. They bought Bear a Power Pal Turbocar.

"These toys are very popular," said the shopkeeper.
"I'm all sold out of Power Pals."

Franklin sighed. "I sure wish I had a Power Pal,"
he said.

"Maybe you'll get one for your birthday," replied
his mother. "It's just a couple of weeks away."

On the day of Bear's party, Franklin wrapped the
Turbocar all by himself. Then his mother handed him
a present wrapped in blue paper.

"Don't forget the gift from Bear's mother," she said.

"That isn't Bear's Power Pal," said Franklin. "It's the
yellow bag in the closet."

"Franklin!" exclaimed his mother. "Did you snoop?"

"Oops," Franklin mumbled.

"Oh, Franklin," said his mother. "The Power Pal is *your* birthday present. I bought it a long time ago. I was afraid there wouldn't be any left."

Franklin jumped up and down.

"Can I have it now? Do I have to wait for my birthday?"

But Franklin's mother had a question.

"Did you tell Bear he was getting a Power Pal?" she asked.

Franklin shook his head.

"I told you I could keep a secret. I told you ..."

Franklin stopped to think.

"I kept the secret from Bear," Franklin finally said. "But I told everybody else. That's why we all bought him Power Pal toys."

"You shouldn't have snooped," said his mother.

"I know," Franklin groaned. "Now everyone will be mad at me. What good are Power Pal toys if Bear isn't getting a Power Pal?"

Franklin slumped in his chair.

"What am I going to do?" he asked.

Franklin was the last to arrive at Bear's birthday party. He joined in the games and ate lots of cake and ice cream. Soon, it was time for presents.

Bear opened his gifts from Beaver and Fox, Snail and Rabbit.

"These are great!" said Bear. "Now all I need is a Power Pal."

Next, Bear opened his mother's gift.

It was a baseball glove. Bear tried it on. Everyone else stared at Franklin.

"There's still my present," said Franklin.

He handed Bear a yellow gift bag.

"A Power Pal!" exclaimed Bear. "It's just what I always wanted!"

Franklin sighed.

"Me too," he said.

Then Bear leaned over to Franklin.

"Don't worry," he whispered. "My mom bought you a Power Pal for your birthday."

"How do you know?" Franklin asked.

"I snooped," answered Bear.